ༀ༔ ། །སྤུན་གྱི་ཁང་ལ་བསྐྱེན་འཛིན་ཚོར་ནུ་ཡིན་ཏེ་གངས་ཅན་ཚིགས་ཁ་ནས་ཞིག་གནས་པོ་ཧྀམ་རྒྱུན་

དང་རང་གི་ལོ་རྒྱུས་མ་འོར་བསྐྱེས་ཞིག་བརྗོད་ནོ། ད་སྐྱེས་ས་ཞི་ཏི་ནུ་ལ་ཡ་རྗེ་རྒྱུན་ཉེ་པོར་ཡུལ་ལུ་

རོལ་པོར་སྦྱ་ལ་ཏིང་ཀུ་ནང་གི་དགོན་པ་བག་གཙུག་བསྐྱེན་འཛིན་གྱི་ཐུར་སྐྱེས། སྟོན་ཕྲིན་ཚེས་རྗེ་གཁས་

གུན་རྣམ་གྱོ་ལ་བཟང་པོ་ཞིས་གྱུ་པ་འོད་དགུས་སུ་སྤོན་གཉེར་མཐར་ཐུན་ཏེ་ཕྱིར་རང་ཡུལ་དུ་ཕེབས་ནས་

གུ་ལུང་དགོན་པ་འདི་ཕུག་བཏབ་འདུག། སྤུར་དགོན་པ་འདི་ནས་ལུ་བརྒྱ་གུགས་ཚན་སྐྱང་ལུང་པ་ཞེས་པ་

ཞིག་ཀྱང་སྐྱེ་ཁོ་གི་ཕྱུགྲ་ནས་རོ་མོ་སྟོན་རྒྱུན་འདི་དོན་པ་དཔར་ཕོས་སྐོལ་རྒྱུན་འཛིན་ཏེ་ངུ་གུས་སུ་ཡོད།

དཔེར་ན༡ གུ་མ་བསམ་གཏན་ནོར་བུང་དུ་༢ གུ་མ་རྗོ་རེ་ཡི་ཤུ༣ གུ་མ་ཨོ་རྒྱན་རྣ་རྒྱལ་ཏེ་ཡི་ཕུན་

གུ་མ་གཙུག་བསྟན་འཛིན་རེས་བུ༤ བདག་བསྐྱེན་འཛིན་ནོར་བུ་བཅུས་རོ་མཁུངས་ལུན་ཞིང་འདོ། ཚུས་

སྐུ་ཚིགས་མཆིས། ཁོ་བོད་སྐབས་བལ་ཡུལ་རྒྱལ་སར་ཀུ་ཏུ་མན་འདུས་སུ་སྤོན་ཕུག་ཚོ་ལྱུན་ད་

རེ་མོ་འདྲོ་བཞིན་འདུགམ། བོད་རྒྱ་ལོ་༢༡༢༥ཡོར་ཟླ༡༢ ཚེས༡༠ལ བོད་ཚོ་ལོ་ཕྱུན་བསྟན་

རྒྱ་མཚོ་ནས་བྲིས། དགེ་ལེགས་འཕེལ།།

First published in English in the United States and Canada 2002 by
Groundwood Books
First published in French in 2000 by Éditions Milan as Himalaya: L'Enfance
d'un Chef by Tenzing Norbu Lama
French text by Justine de Lagausie, from an original sceenplay by Eric Valli
and Olivier Dazat, with the collaboration of Jean-Claude Guillebaud, Louis
Gardel, Nathalie Azoulai et Jacques Perrin
Translation and adaptation by Shelley Tanaka

Groundwood Books / Douglas & McIntyre
720 Bathurst Street, Suite 500, Toronto, Ontario M5S 2R4

Distributed in the USA by Publishers Group West
1700 Fourth Street, Berkeley, CA 94710

National Library of Canada Cataloguing in Publication Data
Tenzing Norbu, 1971-
Himalaya
ISBN 0-88899-480-X
Dolp. (Nepal)—Juvenile fiction. 2. Dolp.
(Nepal)—In art. I. Title
PZ7.T3589Hi2002   j843   C2002-900521-3

Library of Congress Control Number: 2002102922

Printed and bound in China by Everbest Printing Co. Ltd.

TENZING NORBU LAMA

Himalaya

A GROUNDWOOD BOOK • DOUGRONTO VANCOUVER BERKELEY

The fields of barley waved in the gentle breeze. Tsering gathered up a sheaf of feathery stalks.

"Look, Grandfather," he said. "There's enough here to feed our village for a whole lifetime. No one will be hungry this winter."

Old Tinle laughed. "The harvest is good, but it's not enough," he told his grandson. "We'll need to go down into the valley again to trade for more grain if we're to have enough to last through the winter."

Tsering's father, Lhapka, was the village chief. He had been away for several weeks, guiding an expedition over the high plateaus to collect salt. When he returned, he would lead a caravan of yaks down the steep mountain passes to trade the salt for grain.

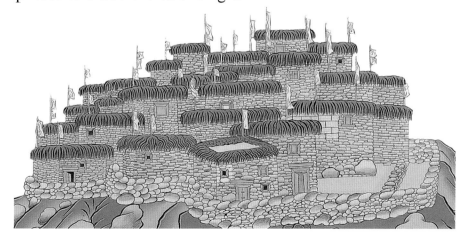

Tsering missed his father. He couldn't wait for him to return.

As the boy walked home, he felt the earth shaking.

"Grandfather, it's the caravan!" he shouted. "The caravan's coming!"

The villagers rushed to the foot of the village.

In a cloud of dust, the herd of yaks drew closer. The thundering of their hoofs made the air tremble. But as the dust cleared, Tsering saw a terrible thing. His father's body lay dead on the back of the lead yak. Tsering's mother collapsed in sobs of grief.

The young man Karma was at the head of the caravan. He stepped forward.

"Lhapka fell to his death looking for a shortcut through the mountains," Karma explained. "I told him it was too dangerous, but he wouldn't listen."

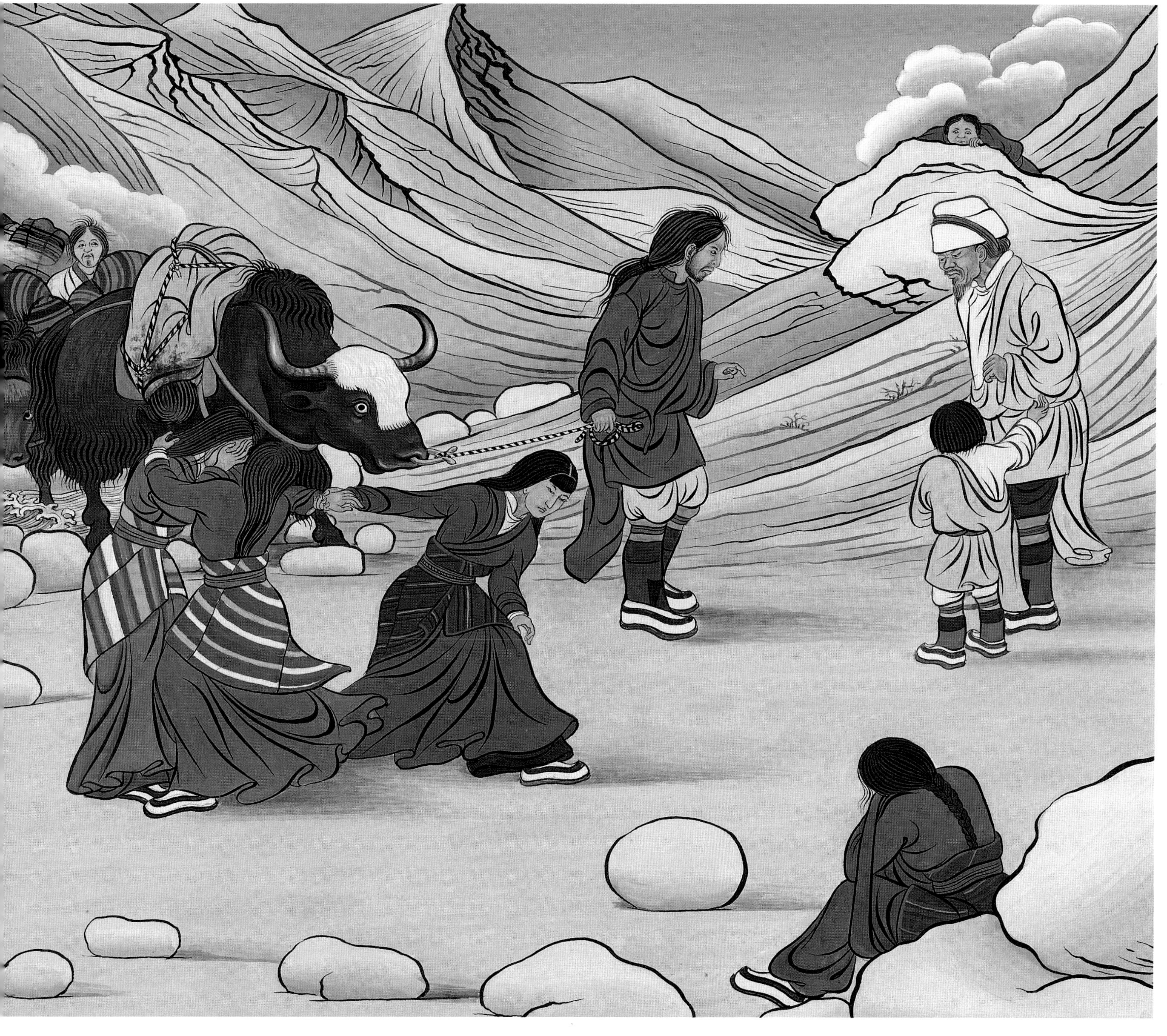

གཡག་
འཁྱུལ་
ཚོ་
ཁྱིར་
འོང་
པ།

Tinle erupted in anger.

"You are a liar!" he shouted. "You have always been jealous of Lhapka. You want to be the new chief. You killed my son on purpose!"

Karma shook his head sadly. "Lhapka was my best friend," he said to the villagers. "I would never hurt him."

Back at home, Tinle declared, "If Lhapka is dead, then his son Tsering should be the new leader. Until he is old enough, I will lead the caravan to the valley myself. I just need a strong young man to help me."

But Tinle could not persuade any of the young men of the village to go with him.

"Karma should be the chief now," they said. "He's the bravest of us all. When he draws his bow, the arrows always fly straight and true."

ནུ་ གཡག་ འབྱལ་ པ་ རྒྱུ
ཆེན་འཆུ་ པ་ ཆེན་ དགོ

Tinle knew that the wise lamas of the village had decreed that the salt caravan should leave for the valley in exactly ten days. He knew he had time.

Tsering was frightened when his grandfather took him to the blacksmith's tent that stood outside the village.

Why would his grandfather take him to the village wizard? Would he really have to lead the caravan in his father's place?

"Come and sit beside me," the blacksmith beckoned. Tsering stepped forward nervously. When he sat down, the man slipped a small pendant in the shape of an anvil and hammer around his neck.

"Wear this, and the evil demons will leave you in peace when you travel to the south," he explained.

Tsering was relieved. He banged the little anvil with the hammer.

Beside him, Tinle smiled.

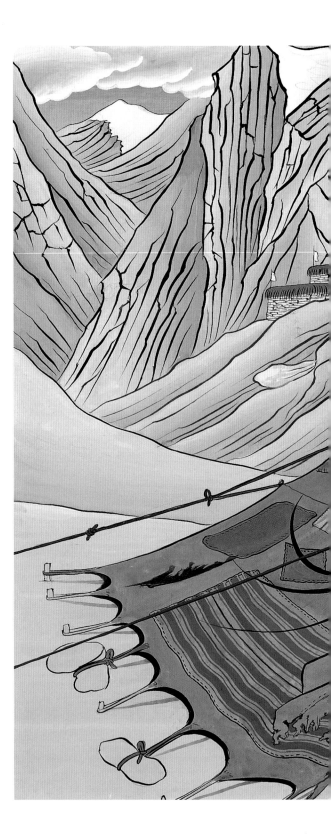

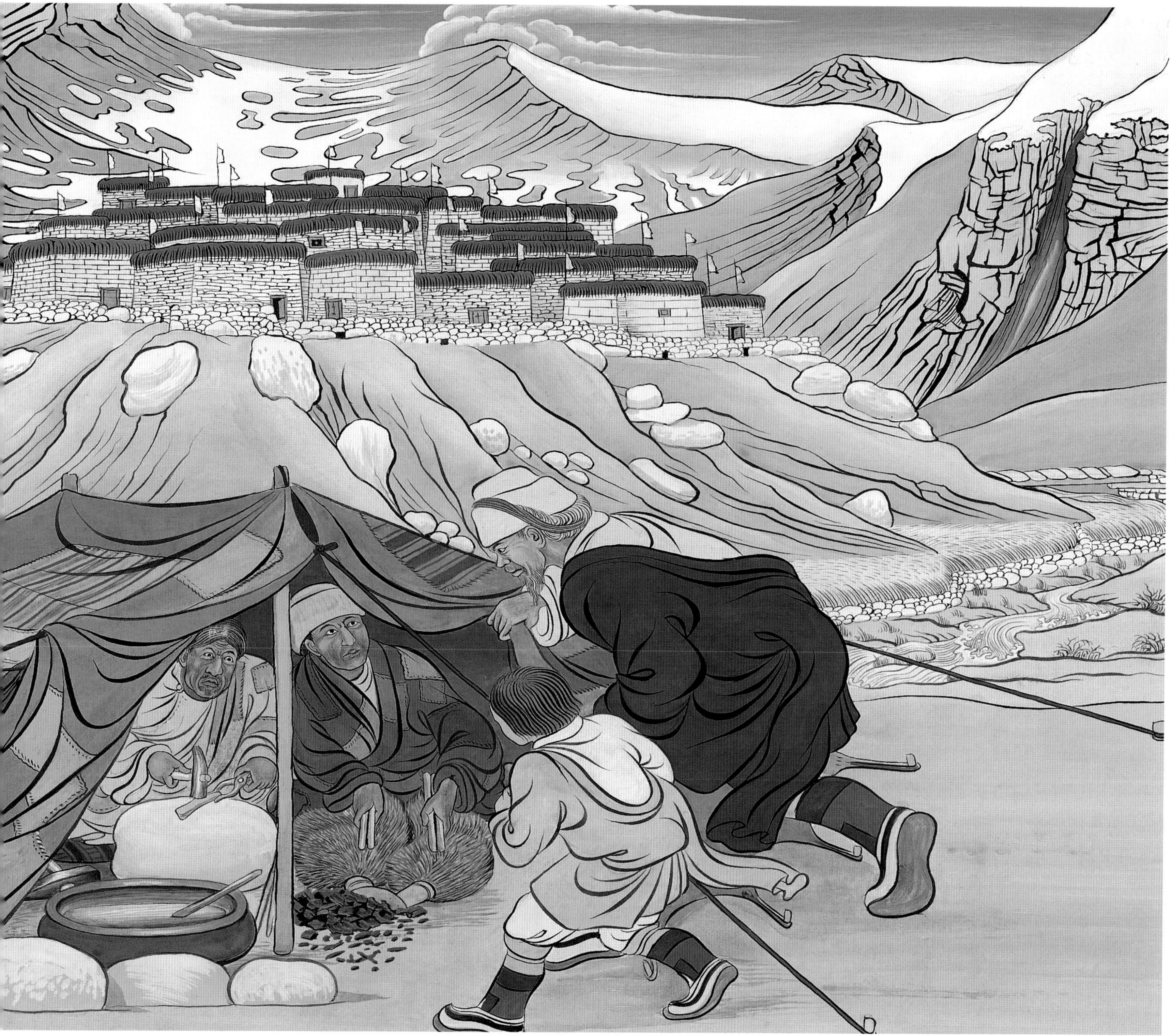

ཚེ་རིང་མིང་པ་མངས་ལ་བསྐྱུར་སོ།

བོད་བུ་དགོན་པ་ནད་སྨན་སྲབས།

At dawn the next day, Tinle mounted his horse and left the sleeping village. He journeyed for two long days until he arrived at the monastery where his younger son, Norbu, had been studying since he was a boy.

Norbu was a lama. He spent his days painting large murals that celebrated the glory of Buddha.

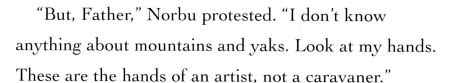

"I have come to fetch you," Tinle told Norbu. "Your older brother, Lhapka, is dead. Until Tsering is old enough, you must lead the caravan."

"But, Father," Norbu protested. "I don't know anything about mountains and yaks. Look at my hands. These are the hands of an artist, not a caravaner."

"Are you afraid?" asked Tinle.

"Not afraid to say no," Norbu replied.

Disappointed and angry, Tinle turned on his heels and left without even saying goodbye.

Meanwhile, back in the village, Karma was getting the caravan ready to leave. He did not want to wait ten days. Winter was fast approaching, and the mountain passes would soon be blocked with snow.

The village people were divided. The older ones wanted him to wait, but Karma managed to convince most of the young people to go with him. They rounded up their yaks in the grazing pastures and loaded them down with cloth bags filled with salt.

When everything was ready, Karma gave the signal. Men, women and yaks headed for the trail, their hoofs clattering on the stones.

From the terrace of his house, Tsering watched them leave, his heart full of sadness.

གཙོ་
གཡུག
ཆུང་
བུས་
ཉམ་
ཚོ་
ཡོངས།

འཕྲིན་
ཡིག་
བོད་
གསལ་
ཤུག་ཡིག
རོང་
པ།

Two days passed. The village was dark and quiet. Suddenly, a voice rang through the night.

"It's Tinle! He's back!"

The villagers came out of their houses and went to meet him. They told him that Karma's caravan had already left with the young men of the village.

"What?!" Tinle roared. "And what about the salt? Where is the salt?"

"We kept our own salt," said the old men. "But what are we going to do?"

"We will do as we have always done," Tinle replied. "We will leave on the day that the wise ones have advised."

A murmur of disbelief went through the group. How could a caravan of old men and women cross the Himalayan mountains?

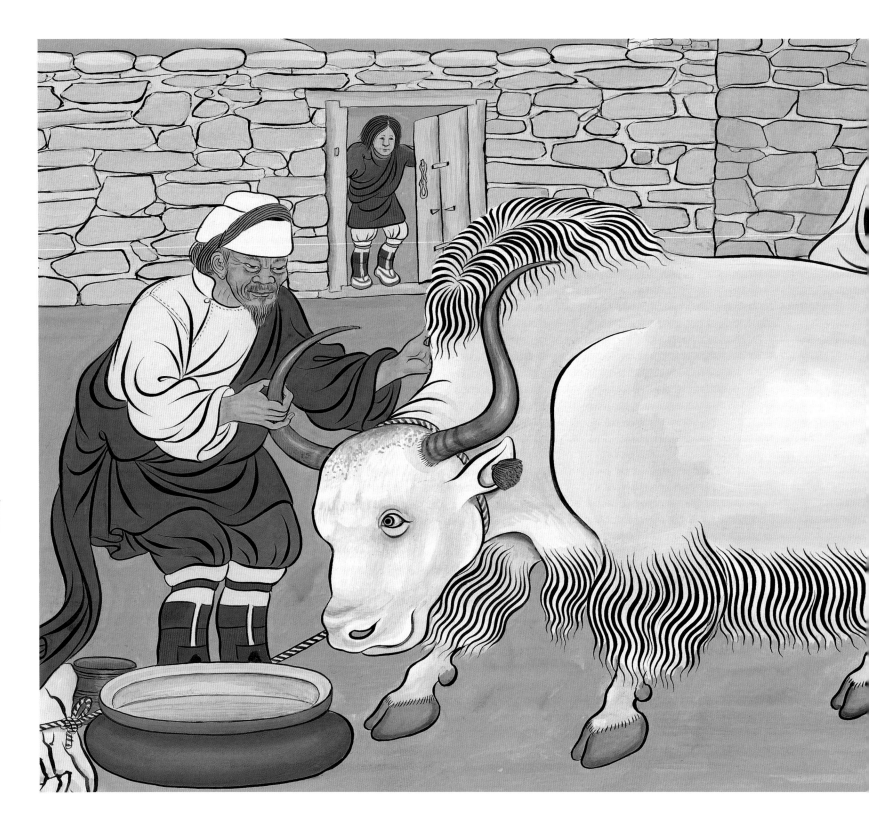

ནོར་
བུ་
དགོན་
པ་
ནས་
རང་
ཁྱིམ་
ད་
འཁྲིད།

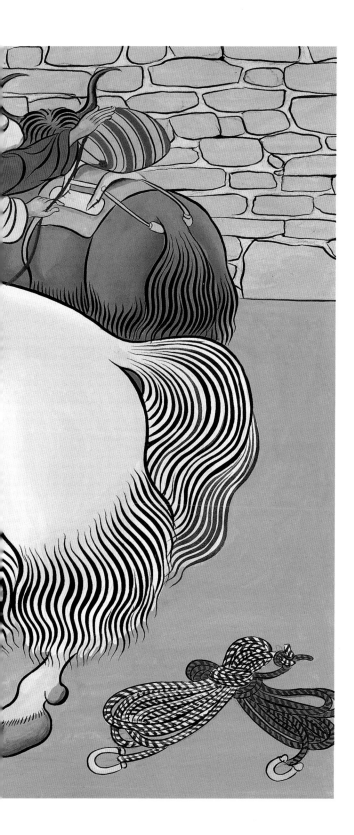

Indeed, it had been a long time since the old ones of Dolpo had driven a caravan. The weight of the years had left them frail and bent, but Tinle gave them back their taste for adventure. He gave them back their courage and pride.

"You are true caravaners," he told them. "That is far more important than being young."

Tsering watched how his grandfather talked to his old white yak while he smeared the animal's horns with red earth, as the chiefs had always done before every journey. Then Tsering helped his mother and his grandmother strap the bags of salt to the backs of the yaks.

Suddenly Tsering looked up.

Standing in the yard was a young man dressed in red and saffron yellow. It was Norbu. The lama had changed his mind.

འཕུན་
ཡས་
ཆུས་
གཡས་
བཙུམ་
གཡོན་
དུ་
ཕྱོན་
པ།

The following day, the second caravan was on its way. Tinle walked at the head, followed by the old men and women of the village. Tsering walked at the back with his mother and uncle, trying to make the herd move more quickly. His face shone with excitement. It was the first time he had traveled with the caravan.

But it was a long day of walking for his small legs.

"Grandfather, my feet hurt. Are we going to walk like this tomorrow, too?"

"Tomorrow and for many days after, my boy. Soon your legs will be as strong as a yak's horns. Then you'll be a true Dolpo-pa."

Day after day, the little caravan followed Tinle.

"We keep walking but we never arrive," Tsering complained. "I want to go home."

"Please, we must go back," Tsering's mother begged. "He's only a child."

Tinle pointed at Tsering, who had suddenly run ahead.

"Yesterday he was a child," he told Tsering's mother. "But one day he will lead the caravan. A true Dolpo-pa never turns back. He is learning what he needs to know."

The old caravaners were finding it harder and harder to keep up.

"Are you trying to kill us, Tinle?" they cried.

"Grandfather, look!" Tsering shouted, pointing toward the top of the mountain. "It's Karma and his caravan! There they are!"

"No, those are just pilgrims."

"What are pilgrims?"

"Religious people who walk," the old man replied.

To his great disappointment, Tinle learned from the travelers that Karma's caravan was five days ahead. He had already gained a full day on them.

རྡོ་
ཁམ་
རྩ་
ཅུང་
སྡུག

ཡམ་
ལས་
དགའ་
 རྒྱན་
དང་

ཆུ་
སྲིན་
ཡ་
མོག་
ཞུ་བ།

An idea crossed Tinle's mind. "When you are faced with two paths, always choose the most difficult. That's what the master at the monastery teaches. Isn't that so, Norbu? Tomorrow we will take the path by the lake."

"By the lake?" cried his companions, horrified. "But there are evil demons there! We will never get through."

"Are we going to see demons?" Tsering asked excitedly.

"Yes! The lake trail is full of them," answered his grandfather. "And thanks to this shortcut, we'll be able to catch up to Karma."

When the villagers protested, Tinle shouted, "And what are you going to eat this winter? Your salt?"

Norbu shrugged. "Talking to Tinle is like talking to the snow falling," he said.

The caravan left at dawn, taking a narrow path that was cut into the cliff beside the water. Tinle led the way. But soon he had to stop. The path was blocked by a mass of fallen rock.

The yaks snorted, angry at being forced to a halt on the edge of the precipice. They could not turn around on the narrow path. Tsering clung to his mother in terror.

Tinle and an old caravaner set to work. Clinging to the cliff, they rebuilt the path rock by rock.

Finally, Tinle pulled his white yak forward.

"If you come, the others will follow," he said.

After a moment of hesitation, the animal took a step, and soon the other yaks followed. But each step shook

the flimsy bridge a little more. When the last yak stepped onto it, the ground suddenly fell away, plunging the animal over the steep cliff.

Tinle looked back. "A yak and two bags of salt? It's a small price to pay the demons for letting us cross."

འབྲོག་
ལས་
གཡག
ཕྱུན་
དུ་ཕུད
ཕབ།

Karma was resting with his men in a makeshift camp when he saw Tinle's caravan approaching. Tsering was sitting astride the lead yak.

"If I had known you were leaving right after me, I would have waited for you, Tinle," exclaimed Karma.

"I left on the day fixed by the gods," replied the old man with pride. Karma shook his head in amazement.

That evening, Tinle consulted the gods to find out when the caravan should move on. He threw a handful of salt into the fire.

"The salt does not crackle," he announced. "There is moisture in the air, and soon the snow will come. We are all tired, but we must carry on at dawn."

Karma did not believe the old man. "The grass is good here, the sky is clear. We can't listen to a pile of salt," he said. But all the others were listening to Tinle now, and they decided to go with him.

Karma stayed behind with his yaks. One of the villagers looked back.

"Tinle and Karma are exactly the same," he said.

The caravan was making its way through the pass when the snow began to fall.

"Grandfather was right," Tsering said to himself.

As the hours passed, the wind howled and raged, and the snow fell thickly. The men and animals were blinded. Tsering could no longer walk. Norbu lifted him onto the back of a yak, where he huddled under a thick blanket.

Don't stop!" shouted Tinle. "If we

don't make it through the pass today, we will be buried alive under this snow!"

But the yaks and men began to fall behind.

"Keep going," he told the others. "I'll go back to make sure we haven't lost anyone." And he headed to the back of the caravan.

No one saw him collapse in the snow.

"Where is Grandfather?" wondered Tsering uneasily, when they finally reached the camp site.

Norbu was very worried, too. Just as he was about to head back into the blizzard to search for his father, they saw a figure staggering toward them.

It was Karma carrying the old man on his back. He had followed them through the storm and found Tinle half buried in the snow.

Everyone ran forward to help. Tinle slowly opened his eyes. He was alive, but he could no longer walk.

By the next day, when the caravan reached the final pass, Tinle was too weak to go any farther. He held his prayer flag out to Karma and asked him to hang it from the top of the rocky cairn to release his prayers to the gods.

"I wish you were my father, Tinle," said Karma.

"You are too much like me to be my son," said Tinle.

"It's up to you to guide the Dolpo-pa now. Just remember. A chief commands his men, but he receives his orders from the gods." And then he died. Tsering wept.

"Tinle was right," said Karma. "He saw a storm in the blue sky. I saw nothing."

"But if you had left with us you wouldn't have saved him," said Norbu.

Norbu recited the prayer for the dead and stayed with Tinle's body while the caravan slowly made its way down to the valley. At last the long journey was over, and the people of Dolpo would finally be able to exchange their salt for grain.

Tsering's heart was full as he gazed at the new world around him. Everything here was so different from the rugged place where he lived.

He walked through a lush meadow and stopped in wonder. Before him stood a huge tree. It was the first real tree he had ever seen, and he wanted to climb to the top. From there he would be able to see a long way.

He was getting ready to become a chief.

© Éric Valli

This story is set in Dolpo, a remote region of the Himalayas in northwest Nepal. The area is windswept, barren and treeless. The people of Dolpo, the Dolpo-pa, grow barley, their staple food, though the short growing season, poor land and meager rainfall do not allow them to produce enough grain to survive on. They also raise yaks. These huge, hairy animals are slow and stubborn, but they can survive the extreme cold, rugged terrain, poor grazing and thin air of the mountains. They provide wool, hides, yogurt and cheese, and their dried dung is used as fuel.

Every year, the people of Dolpo travel north into Tibet to collect rock salt, a life necessity for all people who live on cereal-based diets. Then the yak caravans make a long trek into the central valleys of Nepal, where the salt is traded for more grain. The journey, which takes them over some of the highest mountain passes in the world and takes several weeks, is often a race against the weather, and a sudden snowstorm can mean death for the entire caravan.

The illustrations in this book were painted by Tenzing Norbu Lama, who was born in 1971 in a little village in Dolpo. Tenzing Norbu grew up in a monastery where he studied painting and prepared to be a lama. The paintings measure almost twenty-six feet (eight meters) long and took six months to complete. Tenzing Norbu was the inspiration for the character of Norbu. He now lives in Kathmandu, the capital of Nepal, but he spends three months of every year in Dolpo.